This Little Tiger book
belongs to:

....

....

....

....

CP/494

000002030276

For my most precious gifts,
Stefani, Asa, Harley, Chloe
BB

LITTLE TIGER PRESS
1 The Coda Centre, 189 Munster Road,
London SW6 6AW
www.littletiger.co.uk

First published in Great Britain 2002
This edition published 2016

A CIP catalogue for this book is available
from the British Library

ISBN 978-1-84869-354-8
Printed in China
LTP/1400/1505/0416

2 4 6 8 10 9 7 5 3 1

LION'S PRECIOUS GIFT

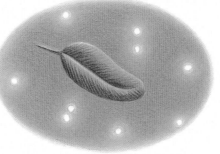

Barbara Bennett
Amanda Hall

LITTLE TIGER PRESS
London

Lion had the most magnificent crown. It was made of the finest gold and was decorated with glittering jewels.

"My crown is the most precious thing in the world," boasted Lion, swishing his thick, silky mane.

"But the world is full of many other magnificent things,"
said Lioness. "If someone brought you an even more
precious gift would you swap it for your crown?"

"Very well then," Lion replied. "Whoever brings me such
a gift shall receive my crown as a prize."

From animal to animal the
message was passed. It was squeaked
and shrieked, croaked and crowed, hooted
and howled. From the shivering South to the
freezing North, from East to West and across
the whole world, news of the competition spread.

What could be more precious than the crown?

That night, every animal dreamed its own dream. Polar Bear dreamed of huge, snowy mountains and vast frozen icicles.

Tiger dreamed of splendid coloured stripes of red and yellow, green and blue.

Eagle dreamed of spreading his wings and flying into the moonlight, to the edge of the sky and back.

Early next morning, Polar Bear
lumbered from her icy cave.
She thundered through snowstorms
and blizzards, and strode over igloos
and icebergs, until she reached the
top of the world.

With a deafening CRACK she
snapped off the tip of the North Pole,
and headed back south towards
the jungle.

That same morning, Tiger threaded his way stealthily between the flowers and the ferns, under the bushes and out on to the grassland.

There, glistening through the bright sun, Tiger saw
a beautiful rainbow arching down to the ground.
With a gigantic POUNCE he snatched the dazzling
stripes from the sky and bounded back to the jungle.

Eagle rested until the night
clouds covered the sky. In the darkness,
he stretched his vast wings and took
off from his nest. Up, up and away he flew,
towering high above the treetops.

Higher and higher the eagle soared,
above the clouds and between the
twinkling stars, until finally he landed
on the moon. With a quick PECK of his
sharp beak, he broke off a piece of
the moon and glided back home.

Polar Bear, Tiger and Eagle were the last to arrive
in Lion's clearing. Many other animals had been
and gone, disappointed, for nothing had been found
to equal Lion's magnificent crown.

"In this bag," said Polar Bear, stepping forward,
"I have the most precious gift! It is the freezing North,
to keep you cool in the heat of the day."

She tipped open the bag, but out spilled two
tiny drops of water. Polar Bear stared in disbelief.
The freezing North was gone!

"Foolish bear," sighed Lion. "Don't you know that
ice melts in hot places? Your gift is quite useless."

Next, Tiger stepped forward.

"My gift is the most precious," he boasted. "In this box I have brought you the stripes of the rainbow. How wonderful you will look, wearing them."

He opened the box, but it was completely empty. Lion tossed his magnificent mane.

"You are even more foolish than Bear," he said. "Don't you know that a rainbow will fade and disappear without the sun and the rain?"

Finally, it was Eagle's turn. He spread his wings and proudly presented his gift at Lion's feet.

"I give you the light of the moon in exchange for the crown," he screeched. "That is the most precious gift!"

Lion gave an enormous roar.
"You are the most foolish creature of all.
Don't you know the moon can only shine
in the evening sky? Here in the jungle it is
nothing but a piece of rock."

Polar Bear, Tiger and Eagle crept away,
shamefaced and disappointed.
As Lion sat in his glittering, sparkling
crown, he felt himself very wise. "Lioness
was quite wrong," he thought. "There is
nothing so precious as my crown. I will
go and tell her so."

Lion padded off across the clearing and through the undergrowth. "Where is Lioness?" he wondered. Before long, from behind the bushes, he heard her deep-throated purr. Lion parted the bushes.

There, in the soft green grass, lay Lioness, and curled
up beside her was their tiny lion cub!

"Look," she purred proudly. "Our baby has been born!"

No jewelled crown could make Lion as proud and happy
as he felt at that moment. As he gently licked and nuzzled
his new-born cub, he laid the crown at Lioness's feet.

"Now I understand," he said. "For what you have given
me is truly the most precious gift of all!"

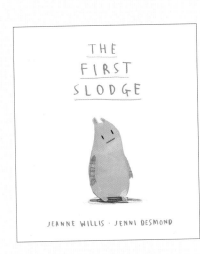
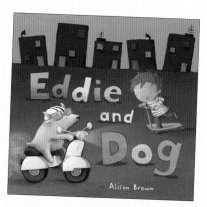

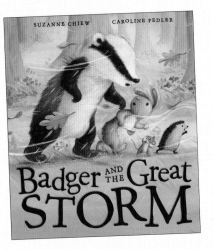

More special stories from Little Tiger Press!

For information regarding any of the above titles or for our catalogue, please contact us:
Little Tiger Press, 1 The Coda Centre, 189 Munster Road, London SW6 6AW
Tel: 020 7385 6333 • E-mail: contact@littletiger.co.uk www.littletiger.co.uk